TIMELESS SHAKESPEARE

JULIUS CAESAR

William Shakespeare

– ADAPTED BY –

Patricia Hutchison

SADDLEBACK PUBLISHING

 **TIMELESS SHAKESPEARE**

www.sdlback.com

Copyright ©2013 by Saddleback Educational Publishing
All rights reserved. No part of this book may be reproduced in any form or by any means, electronic or mechanical, including photocopying, recording, scanning, or by any information storage and retrieval system, without the written permission of the publisher. SADDLEBACK EDUCATIONAL PUBLISHING and any associated logos are trademarks and/or registered trademarks of Saddleback Educational Publishing.

ISBN-13: 978-1-62250-714-6
ISBN-10: 1-62250-714-2
eBook: 978-1-61247-965-1

Printed in Guangzhou, China
NOR/0713/CA21301257

17 16 15 14 13   1 2 3 4 5

— Contents —

	Introduction	6
ACT 1	Scene 1	7
	Scene 2	10
	Scene 3	22
ACT 2	Scene 1	28
	Scene 2	38
	Scene 3	45
ACT 3	Scene 1	46
	Scene 2	60
ACT 4	Scene 1	70
	Scene 2	72
	Scene 3	74
ACT 5	Scene 1	83
	Scene 2	90
	Scene 3	91
	Scene 4	97
	Scene 5	99

Cast of Characters

JULIUS CAESAR Roman statesman and army general

OCTAVIUS Roman statesman; later called Augustus Caesar, first emperor of Rome

MARK ANTONY Roman statesman, general, friend of Caesar.

LEPIDUS Roman politician

BRUTUS, **CASSIUS**, **CASCA**, **TREBONIUS**, **LIGARIUS**, **DECIUS**, **METELLUS CIMBER**, and **CINNA** Plotters against Caesar

CALPURNIA Caesar's wife

PORTIA Brutus's wife

CICERO and **POPILIUS** Senators

— Cast of Characters —

FLAVIUS and **MARULLUS** Public defenders

CATO, **LUCILIUS**, **TITINIUS**, and **MESSALA** Supporters of Brutus

ARTEMIDORUS Teacher

PUBLIUS Old man

STRATO and **LUCIUS** Servants to Brutus

PINDARUS Servant to Cassius

THE GHOST OF CAESAR

A **FORTUNE-TELLER**, **SENATORS**, **CITIZENS**, **SOLDIERS**, **SERVANTS**, **COMMONERS**, and **MESSENGERS**

Introduction

It is 44 B.C. in Rome. Julius Caesar is an army general. He has defeated a rich Roman noble named Pompey. It was a bloody battle. The people are celebrating Caesar's win as the play opens.

Some people who supported Pompey are afraid of Caesar. They think he is greedy for power. They think he wants to become king. This would mean the end of the great Roman Republic. To protect their power, they start to plot against Caesar.

ACT 1

— Scene 1 —

(A street in Rome. **Flavius**, **Marullus**, *and certain* **commoners** *enter.)*

FLAVIUS: Go home, you lazy men. Is this a holiday? Don't you know you can't walk around here doing nothing? You need a sign that tells your trade. Tell me, what is your job?

COMMONER 1: I am a carpenter, sir.

MARULLUS: Where are your tools? Why are you wearing your best clothes? And, you, what do you do?

COMMONER 2: I repair shoes, sir. I mend bad soles. If you are feeling bad, I can fix you.

MARULLUS: What do you mean by that? Are you joking?

COMMONER 2: It's no joke, sir. I can repair your shoes.

FLAVIUS: Why aren't you in your shop? Why did you bring these men onto the streets?

COMMONER 2: To wear out their shoes. Then I'll get more work. Really, sir, we came to join the party. Caesar has won the battle.

MARULLUS: Why are you so happy? What has he won? You have no common sense! Don't you remember Pompey? You often waited all day just to see him. He was a great man. You shouted out with joy when you saw him. And now you celebrate his bloody death. Run home! Fall on your knees! Pray that you will not be punished.

FLAVIUS: Go! Gather all men who feel the same way you do. Go to the river and weep!

*(All the **commoners** leave.)*

See how they vanish. They feel guilty. You go that way toward the Capitol. I'll go this way. Take down any banners that honor Caesar.

MARULLUS: Can we do that? You know it's a feast day.

FLAVIUS: It doesn't matter. Take down the banners. I'll send the commoners home. You do the same. We need to stop Caesar before he becomes too powerful.

*(**Flavius** and **Marullus** leave.)*

— Scene 2 —

*(A public place. The sound of trumpets. **Caesar** enters, followed by **Antony**, **Calpurnia**, **Portia**, **Decius**, **Cicero**, **Brutus**, **Cassius**, and **Casca**. A **crowd** follows, among them a **fortune-teller**.)*

CAESAR: Calpurnia!

CALPURNIA: I'm here.

CAESAR: Stand in Antony's way when he runs by. Antony! Touch Calpurnia as you race past her. Childless women who are touched in this holy race will be able to have children. The elders say so.

ANTONY: I will touch her. When Caesar says "Do this," it is done.

(Trumpets sound.)

FORTUNE-TELLER *(from the crowd)*: Caesar! Beware the Ides of March.

CAESAR: Who said that?

BRUTUS: A fortune-teller warns you to be careful on March 15.

CAESAR: Let me see his face.

CASSIUS: You, come here!

FORTUNE-TELLER: Beware the Ides of March.

CAESAR: He's a dreamer. Let's get away from him.

*(**All** but Brutus and Cassius leave.)*

CASSIUS: Will you go watch the race?

BRUTUS: I'm not interested in sports. But don't let me stop you, Cassius. I'll leave, and you can watch.

CASSIUS: Brutus, you seem to want to stay away from me lately.

BRUTUS: No, Cassius. I've got a lot on my mind. Don't worry about me. I'm sorry. You are a great friend to me.

CASSIUS: I should have asked you sooner. Can you see the great person you are?

BRUTUS: Only by reflection.

ACT 1 | SCENE 2

CASSIUS: Then you can't see how important you are. I've heard many men talking. They say they wish Brutus would take Caesar's place.

BRUTUS: What dangers are you leading me into? You see something that's not in me.

CASSIUS: Brutus, you don't know how great you are. I'll show you things that you can't see about yourself.

(Trumpets and shouting from offstage.)

BRUTUS: What's all this shouting? I'm afraid the people want Caesar to be their king.

CASSIUS *(slyly)***:** Oh, does that bother you? You wouldn't want him to be king?

BRUTUS: I love Caesar. But I wouldn't want him to be king. What do you want to say to me? Is it noble? I'm not afraid to die. I love honor more than I love life.

CASSIUS: I know that. Honor is what I wanted to talk to you about. I would rather die than live under Caesar's rule.

Caesar is no better than you or me. I was born as free as Caesar. So were you. We can do anything he can do. One cold day, he dared me to jump into the freezing river with him. I did. He jumped in after me.

The river was wild. We fought it. Before we could get across, he started yelling, "Help me, Cassius! I'm sinking!" So I carried him to shore.

Now this man has become a god. I must now bow to him! He's a weak man. Once when he was sick, he cried out like a girl. He should not command the respect of the world. He should not be honored.

(Shouts and trumpets from offstage.)

ACT 1 | SCENE 2

BRUTUS: The crowd shouts again! They are calling for more honors for Caesar.

CASSIUS: He acts like he is a giant. We walk under his huge legs, like weak men. We must take our fate into our own hands. It's not destiny's fault that we are slaves. It's our fault. We must not be weak!

Why should Caesar's name be more honored than yours? Your name is as good as his. Why has Caesar grown so powerful? Since when has there only been one famous man in Rome? Can this truly be Rome if there is only one man in it?

BRUTUS: I know you're my friend. And I've already thought about these things. I'll think about what you've said. I'll listen to you. I'll let you know what I think. I do know one thing. If Caesar becomes king, I'm afraid of what it will do to Rome.

CASSIUS: I'm glad my words have had such a great effect on you.

(**Caesar** and his **attendants** enter again.)

BRUTUS: The games are done. Caesar is returning.

CASSIUS: Signal Casca as he passes by. He will tell you what happened today.

BRUTUS: I will. But look, Cassius. Caesar looks angry. Calpurnia is pale. Cicero looks angry.

CASSIUS: Casca will tell us what happened.

CAESAR: Antony!

ANTONY: Yes?

CAESAR: I want fat, satisfied men around me. That Cassius has a hungry look. He thinks too much. He's dangerous.

ACT 1 | SCENE 2

ANTONY: Don't be afraid of him. He's not dangerous. Many men respect him.

CAESAR: I wish he were fatter! I'm not afraid of Cassius. But I don't trust him. He reads too much. He watches things carefully. He understands men's thoughts. He doesn't like plays or music. He seldom smiles.

Men like him are never at ease with someone greater than themselves. That's why they are dangerous. I'm telling you what should be feared. I have no fear. I am Caesar. Come and tell me what you think of Cassius.

(Trumpets sound. **Caesar** *and his* **attendants** *leave, except Casca.)*

CASCA *(to Brutus)***:** Do you want to talk to me?

BRUTUS: Yes. What happened today? Why did Caesar look so sad?

CASCA: Antony offered him a crown. He pushed it away three times. The people shouted. Each time he pushed it off more gently. I could tell he really wanted to take it. He hated to take his fingers off it. The crowd shouted louder. Then he fainted and fell down.

CASSIUS: He fell?

CASCA: Right in the marketplace. He foamed at the mouth. He couldn't talk.

BRUTUS: He must have the falling sickness.

CASSIUS: No, Caesar doesn't have the falling sickness. But honest men like us have it.

CASCA: I don't know what you mean by that. I only know that Caesar fell down.

BRUTUS: What did he say when he came to?

CASCA: Before he fell, he saw that the people were glad he pushed the crown away. So he offered them his throat to cut. Then he fell. When he came to, he asked if he had done anything strange. He wanted them to think he fell because of his illness. Some women cried out, "What a good soul!" They forgave him. If Caesar had stabbed their mothers, they would have forgiven him.

BRUTUS: And then he came away looking sad?

CASCA: Yes.

CASSIUS: Did Cicero say anything?

CASCA: Yes. He spoke Greek.

CASSIUS: What did he say?

CASCA: I couldn't understand him. Some were smiling and nodding their heads. And I have more news. Marullus and

Flavius have been punished. They were caught pulling down banners that praised Caesar. I have to go.

CASSIUS: Will you dine with me tonight, Casca?

CASCA: No, I have other plans. I will another time.

CASSIUS: Tomorrow?

CASCA: Yes, if I'm still alive. And you still want to.

CASSIUS: Good. I will expect you.

CASCA: Good-bye to you both.

(***Casca** leaves.*)

BRUTUS: I have to go too. I'll get in touch with you tomorrow.

CASSIUS: Until then, think of Rome.

ACT 1 | SCENE 2

*(**Brutus** leaves.)*

CASSIUS: Well, Brutus, you are noble. But you might be swayed from honor. We must stick together. Caesar resents me, but he loves Brutus.

Tonight I'll throw letters in his window. I'll make it look like they came from different people. They'll tell Brutus that the people think highly of him. Then I'll tell about Caesar's greed for power.

Caesar had better watch out. We'll take him down! If we don't, Rome will be ruined.

*(**Cassius** leaves.)*

— Scene 3 —

(A street in Rome. Thunder and lightning rumble and flash. **Casca** *enters from one side. His sword drawn.* **Cicero** *enters from the other side.)*

CICERO: Good evening, Casca. Did you bring Caesar home? Why are you out of breath? Why are you staring?

CASCA: I have seen terrible storms. I have seen raging winds break trees. I have seen the ocean rise as high as the clouds. But tonight the storm drips fire! I've never seen that before. There must be a war raging in heaven. The world has angered the gods. They are punishing us.

CICERO: What did you see?

CASCA: A slave held up his hand. It was on fire! But his skin wasn't burned. I met a lion roaming near the Capitol. It watched me walk by. I saw a hundred scared women. They swore they saw men on fire walking in the streets! Yesterday, I saw an owl in the marketplace at noon. I believe these are bad omens.

CICERO: It's a strange time. But these signs might not mean what you think. Will Caesar come to the Capitol tomorrow?

CASCA: Yes.

CICERO: Good night, Casca. Go home and rest. Get off the streets on this wild night.

CASCA: Good night, Cicero.

*(**Cicero** leaves. **Cassius** enters.)*

CASSIUS: Who's there?

CASCA: A Roman.

CASSIUS: I know it's you, Casca.

CASCA: What a night this is!

CASSIUS: I know a man who is like this night. He thunders and roars. He's a man no better than you or me. But he's as fearful and powerful as this strange night.

CASCA: You mean Caesar, don't you?

CASSIUS: I won't say it outright. But Rome is in trouble! We are acting weak.

CASCA: The senators will make Caesar king tomorrow. He will rule all the land.

CASSIUS: I know where I'll put this knife, then.

(He points his knife at his own chest.)

I won't live as Caesar's slave. I'll end my life if I have to. I can set myself free.

(Sounds of thunder.)

CASCA: So can I. Caesar can't makes us his slaves. We all have the power to end it.

CASSIUS: Why should Caesar be a tyrant? He sees that we Romans are weak. You can start a roaring fire with weak straws. Rome will be ruined if we let him rule. I might be in danger telling you how I feel. But I am armed. I am not afraid of danger.

CASCA: I'm not a snitch. I agree with you.

(They shake hands.)

Be firm. I'll go along with you.

CASSIUS: It's a deal. I've gathered some of Rome's most noble men. We're planning something dangerous. But it's the right thing to do. This work is bloody and terrible. The men are waiting for me now.

*(**Cinna** enters.)*

CASCA: Stand close. Someone's coming.

CASSIUS: It's Cinna. He's a friend. Cinna,

where are you going?

CINNA: I came to find you. Who's that?

CASSIUS: It's Casca. He's with us.

CINNA: That's good. What a fearful night!

CASSIUS: Are the others waiting for me?

CINNA: Yes, they are. I wish we could get Brutus on our side.

CASSIUS: Don't worry. Take these letters. Scatter them where Brutus will find them. Then meet us at the usual place. Are the others already there?

CINNA: All but Metellus Cimber. I'll do what you told me.

(Cinna leaves.)

CASSIUS: We'll get Brutus on our side.

CASCA: That would be great. People will

think our actions are evil. But if Brutus joins us, they will think we're doing the right thing. People think highly of Brutus.

CASSIUS: Yes, you're right. Let's go. It's late. At dawn, we'll talk to Brutus. We will make him ours.

*(**Cassius** and **Casca** leave.)*

Act 2

— Scene 1 —

(**Brutus** *enters his garden with* **Lucius**.)

BRUTUS: Go to my study. Bring back a candle.

LUCIUS: Okay. I will.

(**Lucius** *leaves.*)

BRUTUS *(aside)*: How can Rome be saved? Caesar must die. I have nothing against him. But what about the general good? He wants to be king. A crown might change him. He'll be dangerous. He'll have too much power.

The people are his ladder. They'll help him climb to greatness. Then he'll turn his back on them. He's like a snake's egg.

Once he's hatched, he'll be deadly. So we must kill him in the shell.

*(**Lucius** enters again.)*

LUCIUS: I found this letter in your study, sir.

(Lucius gives Brutus the letter.)

BRUTUS: Isn't tomorrow the Ides of March?

LUCIUS: I don't know.

BRUTUS: Go look at the calendar. Let me know.

*(**Lucius** leaves.)*

BRUTUS: Shooting stars give me light to read by.

(He opens the letter and reads.)

"Brutus, wake up! See yourself! Help Rome! Wake up!"

I have gotten many letters like this one. Do they want my help? Oh, Rome, I will help you!

*(**Lucius** enters again.)*

LUCIUS: Sir, tomorrow is March 15.

(Knocking is heard from offstage.)

BRUTUS: Good. Go answer the door.

*(**Lucius** leaves.)*

I have not slept. I keep thinking about what Cassius said. He spoke against Caesar. I've decided to do something terrible. Now everything feels like a nightmare. I am fighting my own conscience.

*(**Lucius** enters again.)*

LUCIUS: Cassius and some others are here.

BRUTUS: Let them enter.

*(**Lucius** leaves.)*

They are plotters. Oh, this secret plan! We should be ashamed. We act like we are Caesar's friends. But it must be done.

*(The plotters, **Cassius**, **Casca**, **Decius**, **Cinna**, **Metellus Cimber**, and **Trebonius** enter.)*

CASSIUS: Hello, Brutus. Did we wake you?

BRUTUS: I've been awake all night. Do I know these men?

CASSIUS: Yes. They all think highly of you. We wish you felt the same way about yourself.

BRUTUS: They are all welcome here. Give me your hands.

CASSIUS: Let's make a pact.

BRUTUS: We won't take an oath. We have given our word. We have a great bond. We'll do it. Or we will die. Oaths are for cowards. We'll do it for Rome. There is no greater cause. We won't break our promise. If we do, Romans will die for no good reason.

CASSIUS: Should we ask Cicero?

CASCA: We shouldn't leave him out.

METELLUS: Yes, we'll ask him. He's very wise. People think highly of him. Our fellow Romans will believe in our cause if he joins us.

BRUTUS: Don't include him. He's not a follower. He will ruin our plan.

ACT 2 | SCENE 1

CASSIUS: Then leave him out.

DECIUS: Shall we only kill Caesar?

CASSIUS: I think we should kill Mark Antony too. Caesar loves him. If Antony lives, he could hurt us later. They should die together.

BRUTUS: It seems too bloody. Antony is only a follower of Caesar. We are not butchers. I wish we could take Caesar's power without killing him. But there is no other way.

Let's kill him boldly, but not in anger. People will see that it was a good thing. They won't think we did it out of envy. We will be called cleansers, not murderers. Don't think of Mark Antony. He won't hurt us once Caesar is dead.

CASSIUS: He could be dangerous. He loves Caesar very much.

BRUTUS: Cassius, don't fear him. If he loves Caesar, he may kill himself. But I don't think he will. He enjoys life too much.

TREBONIUS: There's no reason to fear Antony. Let him live. He will laugh at this later.

(A clock strikes.)

BRUTUS: It's time to go.

CASSIUS: We don't know if Caesar will come out today. The terrible things going on have scared him.

DECIUS: I can talk him into coming to the Capitol.

CASSIUS: We'll all bring him there.

BRUTUS: By eight o'clock. Is that the time?

CINNA: At the latest. Do not fail.

METELLUS: Ligarius hates Caesar. He loved Pompey. Why didn't we think to ask for his help?

BRUTUS: Go get him. I'll ask him.

CASSIUS: It's time to go. Remember what's been said. We are true Romans.

BRUTUS: We must act happy. We can't give clues as to what we're up to. Good morning to you all.

*(All leave but Brutus. **Portia** enters.)*

PORTIA: Hello, Brutus.

BRUTUS: Portia, why are you up so early?

PORTIA: I'm worried about you. Why do you look so sad?

BRUTUS: I'm not feeling well.

PORTIA: Are you sick? Then why are you up? The night air will make you worse. You should be in bed. No, something else is wrong with you. I have the right to know. Please tell me what it is. Who were those men? I couldn't see their faces.

BRUTUS: Please don't worry about me. I'll tell you about it later.

*(A knocking is heard from offstage. **Portia** leaves. **Lucius** enters with **Ligarius**.)*

BRUTUS: Caius Ligarius, how are you?

*(to Lucius)***:** You can go.

*(**Lucius** leaves.)*

LIGARIUS: I hear you're going to do something very noble.

BRUTUS: I am.

ACT 2 | SCENE 1

LIGARIUS: You're very brave! This makes me happy. How can I help?

BRUTUS: I'll tell you. Walk with me.

LIGARIUS: I will follow you, even though I don't know where we're going. I trust you.

BRUTUS: Follow me, then.

*(**All** leave.)*

— Scene 2 —

(Caesar's house. Thunder and lightning. **Caesar** *enters in his nightgown.)*

CAESAR: What a wild night! Calpurnia cried out in her sleep, "Help! They murder Caesar!"—Who's there?

*(A **servant** enters.)*

SERVANT: My lord?

CAESAR: Tell the priests to make a sacrifice. Then report back to me.

SERVANT: Right away.

*(**Servant** leaves. **Calpurnia** enters.)*

CALPURNIA: You cannot leave the house today!

CAESAR: I will go! When my enemies see my face, they will vanish.

CALPURNIA: I never believed in omens. But I'm scared. Last night, a lioness gave birth on the street. Graves opened up. Ghosts roamed the city. Blood ran on the Capitol. These things are strange. I'm afraid.

CAESAR: We can't stop the gods. But I will go out. Maybe these signs are not meant for me.

CALPURNIA: These things don't happen when beggars die. They only happen when princes die.

CAESAR: Cowards die many times. The brave only die once. It seems strange that men fear death. It happens when it happens.

*(**Servant** enters again.)*

What do the priests say?

SERVANT: They say you should not go out today. They sacrificed an animal. But they found no heart.

CAESAR: The gods do this to test me. I would have no heart if I stayed home out of fear. So I won't. Danger knows I am more powerful than it! I will go.

CALPURNIA: You are too sure of yourself. You're not thinking. Do not go out today. Say it's my fear that keeps you in. We'll send Mark Antony to the Senate. He'll say you're not well. Please, I'm begging you!

(She kneels.)

CAESAR: All right. I'll humor you. I'll stay home.

(Caesar helps Calpurnia stand up.)

*(**Decius** enters.)*

ACT 2 | SCENE 2

CAESAR: Here is Decius. He'll tell them.

DECIUS: Good morning, Caesar! I've come to bring you to the Senate.

CAESAR: Just in time. Send my greetings to them. Tell the senators I won't come today. "Cannot" is untrue. So is "Dare not." I will not come today. Tell them, Decius.

CALPURNIA: Tell them he's sick.

CAESAR: Would I send a lie? I'm not afraid to tell the truth. Tell them Caesar will not come.

DECIUS: Please tell me why. I don't want them to laugh at me.

CAESAR: It is my will. I will not come. That's enough. But between us, I'll tell you. Calpurnia wants me to stay home. She dreamed she saw my statue dripping blood. Romans came and bathed their hands in it. She thinks it's an evil sign. She begged me to stay home today.

DECIUS: But that's not what it meant! It was a lucky dream. It meant your blood will revive Rome.

CAESAR: Well said, Decius! I think you're right.

DECIUS: The Senate will give you a crown today. If you don't come, they may change their minds. They'll laugh at your reason for not coming. They'll think you are mocking them. They'll think you're afraid. I'm sorry to say these things. My love for you makes me do it.

CAESAR: Your fears seem foolish now, Calpurnia! I'm ashamed I gave in to them. I have to go.

*(**Publius**, **Brutus**, **Ligarius**, **Metellus**, **Casca**, **Trebonius**, and **Cinna** enter.)*

ACT 2 | SCENE 2

PUBLIUS: Good morning, Caesar.

CAESAR: Welcome, Publius. And, Brutus, up so early too? Good morning, Casca, and all of you. What time is it?

BRUTUS: It's just past eight.

*(**Antony** enters.)*

CAESAR: Good morning, Antony. Thank you all for coming for me.

ANTONY: Good morning, noble Caesar.

CAESAR *(to a servant)*: Go inside. Tell them to make some food and drink.

(Caesar turns back to the men): Come closer. I want to talk to you.

TREBONIUS: Of course, Caesar.

(aside): Yes, I will be so near. Your best friends will wish I had been farther away.

CAESAR: Friends, have some wine with me. Then we'll all leave together.

BRUTUS *(aside)*: Your friends are not true. Oh, Caesar! My heart is sad.

*(**All** leave.)*

Scene 3

(A street near the Capitol. **Artemidorus** *enters reading a note.)*

ARTEMIDORUS: "Caesar, beware of Brutus, Cassius, and Casca. Watch out for Cinna. Don't trust Trebonius or Metellus. Decius is not your friend. Neither is Ligarius. They are all against you. Look around you! You think you're safe. That makes their plan easier. May the gods defend you! Your friend, Artemidorus."

I will give Caesar this note. If you read this, Caesar, you may live. If not, the gods are working with the traitors.

*(**Artemidorus** leaves.)*

Act 3

— Scene 1 —

(In front of the Capitol. A crowd, including Artemidorus and the fortune-teller, awaits. Trumpets sound. **Caesar**, **Brutus**, **Cassius**, **Casca**, **Decius**, **Metellus**, **Trebonius**, **Cinna**, **Antony**, **Lepidus**, **Popilius**, **Publius**, *and* **others** *enter.)*

CAESAR: The Ides of March have come.

FORTUNE-TELLER: Yes, but not gone.

ARTEMIDORUS *(offering his letter)***:** Hail, Caesar! Read this!

DECIUS: Trebonius wants you to read his letter first.

ARTEMIDORUS: Caesar, read mine first. It concerns you more than his. Please read it now.

ACT 3 | SCENE 1

CAESAR: What concerns me will be read last.

ARTEMIDORUS: Don't wait. Read it now.

CAESAR: Is this guy crazy?

PUBLIUS: Sir, step aside.

CASSIUS: Why do you want this to be read now? Come to the Capitol.

(Caesar goes forward. The rest follow.)

POPILIUS *(to Cassius)***:** Good luck today.

CASSIUS: With what?

POPILIUS: Good-bye.

(Popilius advances toward Caesar.)

BRUTUS: What did Popilius say?

CASSIUS: He wished me good luck. I think our plot has been discovered!

BRUTUS: Look, he's going up to Caesar. Watch him.

CASSIUS: Brutus, what should we do?

BRUTUS: Calm down. Popilius isn't telling Caesar our plan. He's smiling. Caesar doesn't look worried.

CASSIUS: Trebonius is ready. He's moving Mark Antony out of the way.

*(**Antony** and **Trebonius** leave.)*

DECIUS: Where is Metellus Cimber? It's time to present his concerns to Caesar.

CINNA: Casca, you have to go first.

(They enter the Senate House.)

CAESAR: Are we all ready? Bring me your problems. What must we work on today?

METELLUS *(kneeling)***:** Mighty Caesar, I kneel with a humble heart.

ACT 3 | SCENE 1

CAESAR: Do not bow. It doesn't move me. I won't change the laws. Your brother has been banished for a reason. If you beg, I will kick you away like a dog. I will not change my mind without good reason.

METELLUS: Please let me speak for my brother.

BRUTUS *(kneeling)*: I kiss your hand. I don't want to flatter you. But will you let Publius Cimber come home?

CAESAR: What, Brutus?

CASSIUS *(kneeling)*: Pardon, Caesar! I beg for Publius Cimber's pardon.

CAESAR: I would be moved by this if I were like you. I am not a beggar. I am as constant as the North Star. I am unmoved. I don't change my mind. I'm not like any other man. I will show you. Publius will stay banished.

CINNA *(kneeling)*: Oh, Caesar—

CAESAR: Go away! You cannot move a mountain as strong as me.

DECIUS *(kneeling)*: Great Caesar—

CASCA: Hands, speak for me!

(Casca stabs Caesar. The others also stab Caesar. Brutus is last.)

CAESAR: You too, Brutus? Then fall, Caesar!

(Caesar dies.)

CINNA: Freedom! Caesar's rule is over! Shout it in the streets!

BRUTUS: People and senators, don't be afraid. Don't run. Caesar's desire for power is gone.

CASCA: Go to the stage, Brutus.

ACT 3 | SCENE 1

DECIUS: And Cassius too.

BRUTUS: Where's Publius?

CINNA: Here. He's really confused.

METELLUS: Stand together. Be ready to fight. Some of Caesar's friends may—

BRUTUS: Don't talk about fighting. Publius, don't worry. We won't harm you or any other Romans.

CASSIUS: Go tell them, Publius. Be careful. Don't let them hurt you.

BRUTUS: Poor Publius! We are the ones who should pay for this. We are the ones who did it.

*(**Trebonius** enters again.)*

CASSIUS: Where is Antony?

TREBONIUS: He ran to his house. He was stunned. People are crying. They run like the world is ending.

BRUTUS: We'll find out what fate has in store. We all die sometime.

CASSIUS: We cut short so many years worrying about death.

BRUTUS: We're Caesar's friends. We've done him a favor. He'll no longer fear death. Let's bathe our hands in Caesar's blood. Let's smear our swords. We'll walk out to the marketplace. We'll wave our red swords. Let's cry, "Peace, freedom, and liberty!"

CASSIUS: Let's do it.

(They smear their hands and swords with Caesar's blood.)

Everyone in the future will know us. We gave our country liberty.

DECIUS: What should we do now? Do we leave?

CASSIUS: Yes. Brutus will lead. We will follow. We are the best hearts in all of Rome.

*(Antony's **servant** enters.)*

BRUTUS: Who's coming? A friend of Antony's?

SERVANT *(kneeling)*: Brutus, my master

said to kneel. He sends a message. He says Brutus is wise, brave, and honest. Caesar was mighty, bold, royal, and loving. He loves Brutus and honors him. He feared and honored Caesar.

Antony wants to come here. He wants to know why Caesar had to die. If you tell him, he will honor you. He will follow you. This is what my master says.

BRUTUS: Your master is wise and brave. Tell him to come here. I will tell him what he wants to know. I won't hurt him.

SERVANT: I'll get him now.

*(**Servant** leaves.)*

BRUTUS: I know that Antony will be a friend.

CASSIUS: I hope so. But I fear him.

*(**Antony** enters.)*

BRUTUS: Welcome, Mark Antony.

ANTONY *(seeing the body)*: Oh, mighty Caesar! Are you really dead? Your glories are over.

(Antony turns back to the men): What will you do now? Who else must die? If you want me dead, kill me now. I will die with Caesar. I will die by the swords that killed him. If you think I'm your enemy, do it now. There is no better time to die.

BRUTUS: Antony, don't ask us to kill you! We must appear cruel. You see our bloody hands. You see Caesar's body. But you don't see our hearts. We pity Caesar. His greed for power made us do this. We did it for the good of Rome. But we respect you, Antony. We will not kill you.

CASSIUS: You will have a strong voice in choosing our new leaders.

BRUTUS: Be patient. The people are filled

with fear. We have to calm them. Then I'll tell you why we did this. We loved Caesar, but it had to be done.

ANTONY: I don't doubt your reasons. I wish to shake all your hands.

(They all shake hands.)

You must see me as a coward or a flatterer. I did love Caesar, it's true. Oh, Caesar, it must grieve you to see me shaking hands with your killers. I want to cry! I'm sorry. Forgive me. You are like a deer struck by many hunters. They are covered in your blood. Caesar loved the world. And the world loved Caesar.

CASSIUS: Mark Antony, I don't blame you for praising Caesar. But what does it mean? Can we still count on you?

ANTONY: That's why I shook your hands. I was swayed for a moment when I looked at Caesar. I'll be your friend. Tell me why you thought Caesar was dangerous.

BRUTUS: Our reasons are good. You will be satisfied.

ANTONY: That's all I ask. Please bring his body to the marketplace. I would like to speak at his funeral.

BRUTUS: We will bring him. And you can speak.

CASSIUS: Brutus, may I speak with you?

*(aside to Brutus)***:** Think again about that. People will be moved by Antony's words.

BRUTUS *(aside to Cassius)***:** I'll speak first. I'll say why Caesar had to die. They'll know Antony speaks with our say-so. We want Caesar to have all the honors the dead deserve. It will help us.

CASSIUS: I still don't like the idea.

BRUTUS: Mark Antony, take Caesar's body. You'll speak after I do. Don't blame us in your speech. Say good things about Caesar. Let the people know we're letting you speak. If you won't agree, you won't have anything to do with his funeral.

ANTONY: I can't ask for more than that.

BRUTUS: Prepare the body. Come with us.

*(**All** leave but Antony.)*

ANTONY: Oh, forgive me, dead body! For being kind to your killers. Here is what's left of you. The best man that ever lived. I pity your killers. A great war will break out. It will be bloody. It will be cruel. Caesar's spirit will get its revenge! The dogs of war will be unleashed.

*(Octavius's **servant** enters.)*

SERVANT: Octavius got Caesar's letters.

He's on his way. They told me to tell you—

(He sees the body.)

Oh, Caesar!

ANTONY: Go away and cry. Seeing your sadness makes me want to cry. Where is your master?

SERVANT: He is 20 miles from Rome.

ANTONY: Go and tell him what happened. It's dangerous for him here. Before you go, help me take the body to the marketplace. I will make a speech. We'll see how the people react. Help me. Then go tell Octavius.

*(**Antony** and **servant** leave with **Caesar's body**.)*

Scene 2

*(The Forum. **Brutus** and **Cassius** enter, along with a **crowd of citizens**.)*

CITIZENS: We want answers!

BRUTUS: Then listen to me, friends. I will tell you why Caesar died.

(Brutus goes to the stage.)

CITIZEN 1: Quiet! Let Brutus speak!

BRUTUS: Please listen to all I have to say. Romans, countrymen, and friends! Have respect for my honor. Judge me wisely. I will speak the truth. I loved Caesar as much as you did. But I love Rome more.

If Caesar lived, he would have made us all slaves. Since he is dead, you are free men. I weep for Caesar. I honor him. But he was too greedy for power. So I killed

ACT 3 | SCENE 2

him. Who here wants to be a slave? Who doesn't love their country? Tell me!

ALL: No one, Brutus! No one!

BRUTUS: Then I have not offended you.

(***Antony*** *and* ***others*** *enter with* ***Caesar's body****.)*

Mark Antony brings his body. Antony had no hand in his death. But he will be helped by it. All of you will have a say in the ruling of our country. I killed my best friend for the good of Rome. If you want me to die for it, I will.

ALL: Live, Brutus, live!

CITIZEN 1: Bring him to his house with honor.

CITIZEN 2: Give him a statue.

CITIZEN 3: Let him be Caesar.

CITIZEN 4: Crown him!

BRUTUS: Citizens, let me leave alone. Honor Caesar. We are allowing Mark Antony to speak. Hear his words.

(***Brutus** leaves.*)

CITIZEN 1: Let's hear Mark Antony.

CITIZEN 3: Yes. We'll hear him.

(*Antony goes to the stage.*)

CITIZEN 4: He'd better not say bad things about Brutus.

CITIZEN 1: Caesar was greedy for power. Rome is better without him.

CITIZEN 3: We're lucky to be rid of him.

ANTONY: Gentle Romans—

ALL: Quiet! We want to hear.

ACT 3 | SCENE 2

ANTONY: Friends, Romans, countrymen, lend me your ears! I come to bury Caesar, not to praise him. Brutus told you Caesar was too powerful. If that's true, it was a bad thing. Caesar died for it. Brutus and the others are letting me speak.

Caesar was my friend. He brought money to Rome. He helped the poor. Was that too powerful? Brutus says it was. And Brutus is a noble man. Caesar refused the crown three times. Was he greedy for power? Brutus says he was. And Brutus is a noble man. I am not calling Brutus a liar. I am saying what I know. We all loved Caesar. So we should mourn him.

(He cries.)

I'm sorry. Bear with me. My heart is in the coffin with Caesar.

CITIZEN 1: He makes a lot of sense.

CITIZEN 2: Caesar was not greedy for power.

CITIZEN 3: They shouldn't have killed him.

CITIZEN 4: They must pay for it!

ANTONY: Yesterday, we honored Caesar. Now he is dead. If I wanted to make you angry, I would upset Brutus and Cassius. They are noble men. So I won't do that. I would rather upset the dead. Or you. Or me. Not those noble men.

I found a paper from Caesar. It's his will. If you heard it, you would praise Caesar.

CITIZEN 4: Read the will!

ALL: Let's hear it!

ANTONY: I can't read it. It will make you angry. It's better that you don't know you are his heirs. What good would that do?

CITIZEN 4: Read the will!

ANTONY: I have gone too far. I have upset the honorable men. The men who stabbed Caesar.

CITIZEN 4: Traitors! They were not honorable!

ALL: The will!

CITIZEN 2: Murderers! Read the will!

ANTONY: Will you force me to read it? Gather round the body. Look closely at him. Shall I come down from the stage?

ALL: Come down!

(Antony comes down from the stage.)

ANTONY: Prepare to cry. Look at his cloak. I remember the first time he wore it. It was on a day he won a great battle. Look, here is where Cassius stabbed him. This tear is from Casca. His best friend, Brutus, stabbed him here.

Look at the blood. Brutus burst Caesar's heart. And Caesar fell. Then we all fell. And treason won. Why are you crying? All you're seeing is Caesar's cloak.

(He lifts Caesar's cloak.)

Look at the man. Stabbed by traitors!

CITIZEN 1: Oh, pitiful sight!

ACT 3 | SCENE 2

CITIZEN 2: Oh, noble Caesar!

CITIZEN 1: We'll get revenge.

ALL: Let's find them! Kill them!

ANTONY: I don't mean to stir you up. The men who did this are honorable. I don't know what made them do it. They will give you good reasons.

I didn't come to change your minds. I am not a good speaker. I am a plain man. A man who loved my friend. I only tell you what you already know. But if I were Brutus? And Brutus was Antony? Then he would stir you up. He would convince even stones to seek revenge.

ALL: We'll have revenge!

CITIZEN 1: We'll burn Brutus's house.

CITIZEN 3: Let's go!

ANTONY: Wait! Let me read the will. Here it is. Caesar grants every Roman citizen money. He has also left you all his private land by the river. You can enjoy it forever. Here was a ruler! There will never be another like him.

CITIZEN 1: We'll burn his body in the holy place. We'll set fire to the traitors' houses. Let's go!

CITIZEN 3: Tear down their houses!

(Citizens leave with the body.)

ANTONY: My job is done. Trouble, you have begun. Go where you want.

(A servant enters.)

SERVANT: Octavius is in Rome. He and Lepidus are at Caesar's house.

ANTONY: I'll go straight there.

ACT 3 | SCENE 2

SERVANT: He said Brutus and Cassius rode away from Rome.

ANTONY: They probably heard about how I moved the people. Bring me to Octavius.

*(**They** leave.)*

Act 4

Scene 1

(A house in Rome. Antony, Octavius, and Lepidus are seated at a table.)

ANTONY: All of these traitors will die.

OCTAVIUS: Your brother must die too. Do you agree, Lepidus?

LEPIDUS: I agree. Publius, your nephew, must also die.

ANTONY: Agreed. Lepidus, go get the will. We'll figure out how to reduce what he left the people.

*(**Lepidus** leaves.)*

ANTONY: Lepidus is unimportant. Should he share power with us?

ACT 4 | SCENE 1

OCTAVIUS: You thought he was important. You took his advice about who should live or die.

ANTONY: That was a way to share the blame. He'll do whatever we say. And when we're done, we'll cut him loose.

OCTAVIUS: Do what you must. But he's a brave soldier.

ANTONY: So is my horse. I reward him with hay. I control him. I teach him to fight. To turn. To stop. Lepidus is like that. He's just property. Listen, Brutus and Cassius are raising armies. We must gather our friends. We need to decide what to do.

*(**They** leave.)*

Scene 2

*(An army camp in Greece. A drum sounds. **Brutus**, **Lucilius**, **Lucius**, and **soldiers** enter. Titinius and Pindarus meet them.)*

BRUTUS: Is Cassius near?

LUCILIUS: Yes. And he's sent Pindarus to greet you.

BRUTUS: I accept his greetings. How did Cassius act?

LUCILIUS: He wasn't friendly.

BRUTUS: His friendship is cooling. He's like a horse before a race. He shows great spirit. Makes a brave show. But when push comes to shove? He fails the test. Is his army coming?

LUCILIUS: They'll camp nearby tonight. Some are already here.

ACT 4 | SCENE 2

*(**Cassius** and his **soldiers** enter.)*

CASSIUS *(to Brutus)***:** You have done me wrong.

BRUTUS: I don't mistreat my enemies. So how can I wrong a brother? We shouldn't argue in front of our men. Let's go to my tent. Then you can tell me about it. I'll listen.

CASSIUS: Pindarus, tell the officers to move the men away from here.

BRUTUS: Lucilius, you do the same. No one should come to our tent until our meeting is over. Lucius and Titinius will guard the door.

*(**All** leave.)*

Scene 3

(Brutus's tent. **Brutus** *and* **Cassius** *enter, arguing.)*

CASSIUS: You have wronged me. You accused Lucius Pella of taking bribes. I wrote a letter taking his side. You ignored what I said.

BRUTUS: You were wrong to write it.

CASSIUS: This is not the time to comment on every little offense.

BRUTUS: Some say you are greedy too. I've heard that you sell honors for gold.

CASSIUS: I am greedy? If you weren't Brutus, I would kill you for saying that.

BRUTUS: And if you weren't Cassius, you would have been punished by now.

ACT 4 | SCENE 3

Remember the Ides of March? Didn't we kill Caesar for justice? Should we now be dishonest? I'd rather be a dog than be such a Roman.

CASSIUS: I won't stand for this attack! I'm an experienced soldier. I should make the decisions.

BRUTUS: No, you shouldn't.

CASSIUS: If you care about your health, don't push me.

BRUTUS: I'm not afraid of you. Go make your servants scared. Your temper makes me laugh.

CASSIUS: Has it come to this?

BRUTUS: You say you are a better soldier? Prove it!

CASSIUS: Don't make me angry. I said older not better. Did I say "better"?

BRUTUS: If you did, I don't care.

CASSIUS: Caesar never made me this angry.

BRUTUS: You wouldn't have dared.

CASSIUS: Don't take my love for granted. I might do something I'll regret.

BRUTUS: I'm not afraid of your threats. I am respected. Your threats don't work. I asked you for money. You wouldn't give it. I can't raise money dishonestly. I don't steal from the poor. You wouldn't help pay for my soldiers. I wouldn't have done that to you. I would die first.

CASSIUS: I didn't deny you. The messenger was a fool. He brought back the wrong answer.

You've broken my heart. A friend would accept my faults. Antony and Octavius can have their revenge on me. I am tired of living. I am hated by my brother. I have been scolded like a servant. Here's my dagger.

(He offers his dagger to Brutus.)

Go on, kill me. Kill me as you did Caesar. When you hated him most, you loved him more than me.

BRUTUS: Put away your dagger. My anger comes quickly. And goes away quickly.

CASSIUS: I don't want to be the butt of a joke when you're angry.

BRUTUS: I was angry when I said that.

CASSIUS: You admit it? Let's shake hands.

(They shake hands.)

CASSIUS: I get my temper from my mother. Forgive me.

BRUTUS: I do. Next time, I'll assume it's your mother speaking. I'll leave it at that.

CASSIUS: I didn't think you could get so angry.

BRUTUS: Oh, Cassius. I am so sad. Portia is dead.

CASSIUS: Dead? No wonder you were so angry with me. How did she die?

BRUTUS: She missed me so much. She was worried about this war. She fell into a depression. She swallowed burning coals.

CASSIUS: That's terrible!

BRUTUS: I don't want to talk about it.

*(**Titinius** and **Messala** enter.)*

BRUTUS: Come in! Let's talk about what we need to do.

(They sit.)

Messala, I have news that Octavius and Mark Antony have an army. They are marching toward Philippi.

MESSALA: I heard that too. They've had a hundred senators put to death. They seized their property.

BRUTUS: Do you think we should march toward Philippi?

CASSIUS: I don't think that's wise. The enemy should come to us. They will tire out. We'll be rested and ready.

BRUTUS: But the people here are on our side only by force. The enemy will urge them to join their army. Our forces should march to Philippi. We're strong now. We should take the chance.

CASSIUS: Then let's go.

BRUTUS: We'll rest a bit. Tomorrow we will go.

CASSIUS: This night started off badly. Let's not argue again.

BRUTUS: All is well.

(***All** leave but Brutus, who calls in Lucius and tells him to sleep inside the tent. Lucius falls asleep, and Brutus reads by the light of a candle.*)

BRUTUS: This light is so dim!

(*The **ghost of Caesar** enters.*)

Who's there? My eyes are playing tricks on me. Are you a ghost? You scare me. Tell me what you are.

GHOST: Your evil spirit, Brutus.

BRUTUS: Why are you here?

ACT 4 | SCENE 3

GHOST: To say that you will see me at Philippi.

BRUTUS: Very well. I will see you there.

*(**Ghost** leaves.)*

Now that I have courage, you vanish! I want to talk more. Lucius, wake up!

(Lucius wakes up.)

LUCIUS: Yes?

BRUTUS: Take a message to Cassius. Tell him to lead his forces early tomorrow. We will follow him.

LUCIUS: Yes, sir.

(***They** leave.)*

Act 5

Scene 1

*(The plains of Philippi. **Octavius**, **Antony**, and their **troops** enter.)*

OCTAVIUS: You said our enemies would stay in the hills. But they're coming closer. They'll fight us here at Philippi.

ANTONY: Don't worry. They want us to think they're brave. But they're not.

*(A **messenger** enters.)*

MESSENGER: The enemy is close. We have to do something.

ANTONY: Octavius, lead your troops to the left side of the battlefield.

OCTAVIUS: I'll go right. You go left.

ANTONY: Why are you defying me?

OCTAVIUS: I'm not. But it's what I'm going to do.

*(Drums sound. **Brutus**, **Cassius**, and their **troops** enter with **Lucilius**, **Titinius**, and **Messala**.)*

BRUTUS: They've stopped. They want to talk.

CASSIUS: Stay here, Titinius.

OCTAVIUS: Antony, shall we start fighting?

ANTONY: No. We'll wait for them to attack us. Step forward. The generals want to talk.

(The leaders step toward each other.)

BRUTUS: You want to talk before we fight. Is that right?

ACT 5 | SCENE 1

OCTAVIUS: You are the one who loves words, not us.

BRUTUS: Good words are better than fighting.

ANTONY: That's a nice speech. Just like when you stabbed Caesar. You cried, "Long live Caesar! Hail Caesar!"

CASSIUS: Antony, your words are as sweet as honey. You've stolen from the bees. Now they have nothing.

ANTONY: They still have their sting.

BRUTUS: You stole their buzzing too. And left them silent. But you wisely warn us before you attack.

ANTONY: Yes, I did. But you gave Caesar no warning before you attacked him. You bowed before him. Then stabbed him in cold blood.

CASSIUS *(reminding Brutus that he had wanted to kill Antony on March 15)***:** Brutus, you are the one to blame. If I'd had my way, Antony wouldn't be speaking now.

OCTAVIUS: Arguing will make us sweat. Fighting will make us bleed. I draw my sword against the traitors.

(He draws his sword.)

I won't give up until Caesar's killers have been punished! Or perhaps the traitors will kill me first.

BRUTUS: You are the traitor, Octavius.

OCTAVIUS: I was not born to die by your sword, Brutus.

BRUTUS: It would be a noble way for you to go.

ACT 5 | SCENE 1

OCTAVIUS: Antony, let's go. Traitors, if you have the courage, come to the battlefield and fight.

(**Octavius**, **Antony**, *and their* **troops** *leave.*)

CASSIUS: We are heading for trouble.

BRUTUS: Lucilius, listen. I need to speak with you.

(*Lucilius steps forward. He and Brutus step aside together to talk.*)

CASSIUS: Messala!

MESSALA (*stepping forward*): Yes, General?

CASSIUS: Messala, today is my birthday. Be my witness. I am being forced to fight against my will. I have never believed in omens. Today, I have changed my mind.

Ravens and crows fly over us. They look at us like sickly prey. Their shadows fall over our army. It looks as if we're ready to die.

MESSALA: Do not believe this!

CASSIUS: I'm ready to meet danger.

(Brutus returns with Lucilius)

*(turning to Brutus)***:** Now, Brutus, let's think about what might happen. If we lose this battle, this may be the last time we talk. What do you want to do?

BRUTUS: I always blamed old Cato for killing himself. Only cowards take their own lives. They fear what might happen. I think it's better to face what might come.

CASSIUS: So, if we lose, you won't mind being carried as a trophy through the streets of Rome?

BRUTUS: Never! I will never go to Rome in chains. Let's end this now. I don't know if we'll ever meet again. So let's say our last good-bye. If we meet again, we will smile. If we don't, this is good-bye.

CASSIUS: Good-bye, Brutus.

*(**All** leave.)*

Scene 2

*(Sounds of battle. **Brutus** and **Messala** enter.)*

BRUTUS: Ride, Messala. Give these orders to the men on the other side.

(He hands Messala papers.)

(Loud trumpets sound.)

Let them attack now. I think I see a weakness in Octavius's army. Let them all come down from the hills.

*(**All** leave.)*

Scene 3

*(Sounds of battle. **Cassius** and **Titinius** enter.)*

CASSIUS: Look, Titinius, our soldiers are leaving. This flag-bearer was running away. I killed him. And took the flag.

TITINIUS: Oh, Cassius, Brutus gave the word too early. He was too eager. His soldiers started looting. Now Antony's men surround us.

*(**Pindarus** enters.)*

PINDARUS: Get away from here! Mark Antony is in your tents!

CASSIUS: This hill is far enough. Look, Titinius! Are those my tents burning?

TITINIUS: They are.

CASSIUS: Titinius, be quick! Get on your horse. Ride there and hurry back. Tell me if those troops are friendly.

TITINIUS: I will return quickly.

(Titinius leaves.)

CASSIUS: Pindarus, get higher on that hill. Tell me what you see.

(Pindarus climbs the hill.)

I was born on this day. I will die on this day too.

(to Pindarus, shouting): What do you see?

PINDARUS *(shouting)*: Oh no! Titinius is surrounded by men. He has been captured!

CASSIUS: Come down. Stop looking. My best friend has been taken! I am a coward!

ACT 5 | SCENE 3

(Pindarus comes down from the hill.)

Do you remember the day I took you prisoner? I spared your life. You promised to do whatever I said. You are free now. Take this sword and stab me in the heart.

(Pindarus stabs Cassius.)

CASSIUS: Caesar, this is revenge for your death. I am killed with the sword that killed you.

(Cassius dies.)

PINDARUS: Now I'm free. But I'd rather not be free this way. I'll run far away. No Roman will find me.

*(**Pindarus** leaves. **Titinius** and **Messala** enter.)*

MESSALA: So far, we're even. Brutus won over Octavius. But Antony defeated Cassius.

TITINIUS: Cassius won't be happy about this.

MESSALA: Where is he?

TITINIUS: I left him on this hill with his slave.

MESSALA: Isn't that Cassius lying on the ground?

TITINIUS: He's dead. He must have thought we lost.

MESSALA: What a terrible mistake!

TITINIUS: Where is Pindarus?

MESSALA: Find him. I'll go tell Brutus what happened to Cassius.

TITINIUS: Hurry!

(**Messala** *leaves.*)

Oh, Cassius, didn't you hear the shouts of joy? You're wrong about everything! Brutus gave me this crown for you. I will put it on your head. Cassius's sword, find my heart.

*(**Titinius** kills himself.)*

*(**Messala** enters with **Brutus**, **Cato**, and others.)*

BRUTUS: Messala, where is Cassius's body?

MESSALA: Over there. Titinius is mourning him.

BRUTUS: Titinius is lying face-up.

CATO: He's dead.

BRUTUS: Oh, Caesar, you are still strong! Your spirit walks. It forces us to kill ourselves.

CATO: Titinius was very brave. Look how he crowned Cassius.

BRUTUS: They were both noble men. Good-bye to the last of the noble Romans. I can't cry now. I will find time later to weep for you, Cassius. Send his body home to be buried. Lucilius and Cato, let's go to the battlefield. Before night, we will fight again.

*(**All** leave.)*

Scene 4

*(Another part of the battlefield. Trumpets sound. Then **Brutus**, **Cato**, **Lucilius**, and **others** enter.)*

BRUTUS: Countrymen, be brave!

CATO: Of course we will! I will shout my name in the battlefields. I am Cato, enemy of tyrants!

BRUTUS: And I am Brutus. I am a friend to Rome!

*(**Brutus** leaves. **Antony** and Octavius's **soldiers** enter and fight. Cato falls.)*

LUCILIUS: Oh, Cato, are you dead? You died bravely!

SOLDIER 1 *(to Lucilius)*: Give up or die!

LUCILIUS: I'd rather die. Kill me. I am Brutus.

SOLDIER 2: Tell Antony that Brutus is our prisoner.

SOLDIER 1: Here comes the general.

(***Antony** enters.*)

Brutus is taken!

ANTONY *(looking around)*: Where is he?

LUCILIUS: He's safe. No enemy will take him alive. The gods will defend him. He will never be shamed!

ANTONY *(to Soldier 1)*: This is not Brutus. But he's still a prize. He was posing as Brutus to protect him. Keep this man safe. Be kind to him. I would rather have him as a friend. Go and see if Brutus is alive or dead.

(***All** leave.*)

Scene 5

(Another part of the battlefield. **Brutus** *and* **Strato** *enter.)*

BRUTUS: Come and rest on this rock. We cannot win this fight. Caesar's ghost appeared to me last night. I will die today.

STRATO: Don't say that.

BRUTUS: It's true. Our enemies have beaten us. It would be better for us to kill ourselves than to be killed by them. You're a good man. Will you hold my sword? I'll run myself onto it. Will you do that for me?

STRATO: Give me your hand.

(He holds Brutus's sword.).

Good-bye, my lord.

BRUTUS: Good-bye, good Strato.

(He runs onto his sword.)

Caesar, you can rest now! I didn't kill you half so willingly.

*(Brutus dies. Trumpets sound. **Octavius**, **Antony**, **Messala**, **Lucilius**, and the **army** enter.)*

OCTAVIUS: Who is that?

MESSALA: Brutus's man. Strato, where is Brutus?

STRATO: He is free from the slavery that binds you, Messala. Brutus has killed himself. No one gains honor by his death.

LUCILIUS: That's the way it should be.

OCTAVIUS: I will take all who served Brutus. Come and join me.

STRATO: I will, if Messala okays it.

ACT 5 | SCENE 5

OCTAVIUS: What do you say, Messala?

MESSALA: How did Brutus die, Strato?

STRATO: I held the sword. He ran onto it.

MESSALA: Octavius, take him. He did the last service to Brutus.

ANTONY *(respectfully)***:** This was the noblest Roman of all. All the murderers were jealous of Caesar. But Brutus was not. Brutus acted for the good of Rome. His life was good. Nature will stand up and say to the world, "This was a man!"

OCTAVIUS: He was a good man. Let's bury him with respect. His body will lie in my tent tonight. I will treat him honorably. He was a good soldier. Tell the army to rest. Then we'll go home. We'll share the glories of this happy day.

*(**All** leave.)*